JACK SPLAT

Dog's Dinner

To Sheila and family –
for all the cool bug facts you know! ~ LK

For Alice and Sally ~ AR

STRIPES PUBLISHING
An imprint of Magi Publications
1 The Coda Centre, 189 Munster Road, London SW6 6AW

A paperback original
First published in Great Britain in 2011

Text copyright © Lou Kuenzler, 2011
Illustrations copyright © Andrew Rowland, 2011

ISBN: 978-1-84715-143-8

The right of Lou Kuenzler and Andrew Rowland to
be identified as the author and illustrator of this work
respectively has been asserted by them in accordance with
the Copyright, Designs and Patents Act, 1988.

A CIP catalogue record for this book is available
from the British Library.

Printed and bound in the UK.

2 4 6 8 10 9 7 5 3 1

JACK SPLAT

Dog's Dinner

Lou Kuenzler

Illustrated by Andrew Rowland

Stripes

Chapter One

Do I Nose You?

Hello up there, Buddy!
Yes, you sticking your BIG nose
in this book. It's me, Jack Splat! The
fearless fly hero! Why do you humans
even have such BIG noses, anyway?
Your sense of smell is hopeless
compared to mine. I smell things through
my super-cool wibbly-wobbly antennae.
You should get yourself a pair, Buddy-
Big-Nose! Even something as simple as
a trip to the park is a paradise of
pongs for a superfly like me.

JACK SPLAT

On a hot, sticky summer's day like today, there's nowhere else to be. There are the bins to explore, the sweaty joggers to sniff and, of course, there's dog poo! I was just about to buzz over there in search of a fresh, steaming pile when...

"Where are you going, Jack? Wait for me! Mum said you had to look after me, remember?"

It was my pesky little cousin Flo. She goes on like that all the time, buzzing away in my antennae. (See! I told you my antennae were super cool – I hear through them as well.)

I have about seven thousand four hundred and thirty-six aunts, but Flo's mum, Aunt Emmeline, is my favourite. "Your mum always saves me the best bits of greasy sausage from behind the chip shop," I told Flo. "So I owe her a favour ... even if that means looking after you!"

"I'll be NO trouble, Jack..."

"Just keep quiet and follow me!" I said. "I'll show you round the park."

"You're my bestest cousin!" Flo grinned.

I shouldn't get cross with her really. Until a couple of days ago, Flo was just a tiny, wiggly maggot. Now she's turned into a baby fly, there are so many things that a super-cool big cousin like me can show her!

"Come on," I said, as we flew through the park railings. "I'll give you a tour of all the AWESOME places I know."

JACK SPLAT'S TOP 5 PARK PLACES!

5 The Duck Pond: a bit wet and can be dangerous (look out for fly-eating frogs). Great for soggy bread the ducks don't eat.

(PS look out for ducks, too.)

4 Sandpit: plenty of toddlers and babies here. Little kids are great! All that dribble, dropped food and spilt juice! Yum!

3 Playground: be careful of big kids, but this is where the ice-cream van parks! Cool! (Really cool – the ice lollies are freezing, you don't want to get your feet stuck on one of those!)

2 The Woodland Walk: perfect for squirrels! Even better for squirrel poo or, as I like to call it, Nutty Delight – the snack with a hazelnut in every bite!

1 Litter Bins: these are the treasure chests of the park, full of sandwich crusts and fizzy drink cans. Fly-tastic!

"The very best thing about the park is dog poo!" I told Flo. "But you can't put that on a list of places, because you never know where it's gonna land!"

"How will we find any?" asked Flo.

"With skill and cunning!" I said. "But don't worry! I know everything there is to know about poo. I'm even writing a guide book to the great poos of the world — I call it my Encyclopoodia!"

"That's funny!" Flo giggled.

"No it's not! My Encyclopoodia is a very serious scientific work!" I said.

I swooped high over Flo's head, casting my eyes in all directions.

"The first thing you need if you want to find a nice fresh dog poo," I explained, "is a dog."

JACK SPLAT

"You really are clever!" said Flo. But she was still giggling.

"While we wait for some dogs to show up, let's check out my favourite litter bin," I said.

Now I'd show her something really cool. The best bin in the park is halfway between the ice-cream van (lots of sticky lolly wrappers) and a row of benches where people eat lunch (plenty of half-chewed sausage rolls and soggy tomatoes).

I shot off at top speed.

"Wait for me, Jack!" moaned Flo. "Why do you always fly so fast?"

"If you didn't talk so much, you might fly faster!" I said, as I dive-bombed into the bin.

Digging around in a bin always makes me feel like I've arrived on a desert island – like I'm a pirate searching for buried treasure.

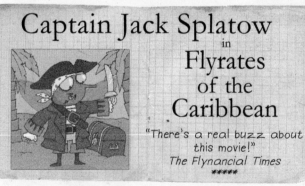

Captain Jack Splatow
in
Flyrates
of the
Caribbean

"There's a real buzz about this movie!"
The Flynancial Times
★★★★★

"Shiver me wing-tips!" I growled. "There's hardly anything here. Some interfering do-goody human must have emptied this bin!"

But Flo had spotted a few soggy crumbs of blueberry muffin floating in some frothy coffee dregs. She flew down inside the paper cup to throw up on them. (That's how we flies eat. We don't have teeth, but with the POWER OF PUKE our stomach juices melt anything into a nice slurpable mush we can suck up through our long proboscis mouths!)

"The blueberries are turning my puke purple," she said. "Look!"

I peered over the brim of the cup.

And WHAM! Something hit me on the back of the head and sent me flying into the cup below. A bag of dog poo had come hurtling into the bin!

"Ouch!" I cried. "I was so busy staring at your pesky purple puke,

I never saw that coming." Even r...
backwards vision and super-sensitiv...
radar hadn't picked up the bag until
it was too late.

"Great!" I paddled through the cold
coffee dregs and looked up to where
the blue plastic poo bag was wedged
into the rim of the cup, stopping the
air from getting in. "Our escape route
is blocked. Five minutes and we won't be
able to breathe in here."

"'Help!" Flo screamed, her voice echoing round the cup. "Are we going to die? How will you save us, Jack?"

MY ENCYCLO**POO**DIA™
A–C

A is for Aardvark Poop – these cunning creatures bury their poo like manure, so the fruit they eat will grow quicker. Aard work … but it's worth it!

B is for Bottoms or Bums – the centre of all poo business. Humans have pretty big ones. The *gluteus maximus* (or buttock muscle) is the biggest in the human body!

C is for Cow Pats – a fresh meadow feast! The average cow poops up to 100lb a day. That's like 100 cans of baked beans each! UDDERLY brilliant, I say!

Chapter Two
It's in the Bag!

The poo bag was blocking the top
of the cup like a tight plastic lid.
I crawled up to investigate, but there
wasn't even a tiny gap round the side.

"Help!" wheezed Flo. "What are we
going to do now?"

Typical! She's the one who gets us
trapped in here ... and I'm the one who
has to get us out.

"My feet are wet!" she moaned.
"I want to go home. I want my mum!"

"Try to BE QUIET!" I said. "And I'll
think of a super-cunning plan."

What we needed was some sort
of poop scoop. Good plan. No scoop.

Or a giant mechanical claw...

"Have you thought of anything
yet?" whimpered Flo.

"How can I think with you buzzing
in my antennae?" I sighed. "It's like
being stuck in a jam jar with a
swarm of fruit flies!"

Flo made a gulping sound like a
frog's burp.

"Don't cry," I snapped. "It's your
fault we're trapped in the first place!"

"I only wanted to show you my
pretty puke..." Flo's sobs got louder.

"Shhh!" I said. "I'm trying to think.
Even a genius like me needs peace and
quiet. Now where was I? A giant
mechanical claw? Good plan. But no—"

"I have an idea," said Flo. "It's probably rubbish..."

"A rubbish idea is perfect!" I said. "We are stuck in a bin, after all!"

"I won't help if you tease me!" she sniffed.

Her? Help? I'm a superfly who has faced untold perils and adventures – until two days ago Flo didn't even have wings!

"Go on," I said. "Let's hear it."

Anything had to be worth a try. I followed her up the cup and on to the bag.

"Let's jiggle our bums," said Flo. "And wriggle our legs. And..."

"Ow!" I said, as she kicked me in the guts.

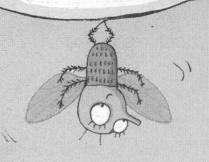

Flo looked ridiculous — like she was trying to do fly ballet or something.

But as she danced, the plastic bag above us began to rustle and move.

It was working! She might look soppy, but it was actually a pretty smart idea.

"Right," I said, taking control of the situation. "Keep wriggling close to the rim of the cup. We should be able to lift the bag just enough to crawl out."

"That's what I am doing!" said Flo. "That was my idea!"

"Well... You're not kicking hard enough," I said. "You're twirling around

like some soppy fly ballerina. Like
Darcey Buzzell, or something! You
need to give it a good, strong kick.
Imagine you're Flyonel Messi or Wayne
Flewney aiming for goal."

With all my might, I booted the
round poo inside the plastic bag.

It didn't budge.

But as Flo did another of her soppy
ballet moves – pointing all six of her
feet – the whole bag slithered off the
edge of the cup.

"See!" she cried triumphantly.

"It's only because I loosened it for
you!" I said.

We crawled out of the coffee cup and gulped the smelly air of the bin. The plastic bag lay harmlessly beside the cup and I went over to investigate.

"If only we could get inside there!" I said. "Why do humans have to scoop up poop anyway?"

I climbed up the poo bag, waving my antennae to try to get a good sniff at least.

"Ah ha!" I cried, as I reached the top. My super-sensitive senses had caught a whiff of something...

"There's a hint of sardine." I wriggled my antennae again, as Flo crawled up beside me. "And sausage. And, strange ... what's that last smell? Something cheesy..."

"Smells like feet to me!" said Flo.

"Don't be ridiculous, Flo! How can a poo smell of feet!"

Flo looked hurt. "The dog might have eaten a pair of socks?"

She was right!

"A lucky guess!" I said. "Sardines, sausage and socks! This poo smells like a perfect three course meal!"

MENU *of* POO!

Starter:
Sardines

Main course:
Sausage

Pudding:
Smelly socks

(It's always nice to finish with a little cheese.) DELICIOUS!

"I – Jack Splat – have found the Perfect Lump of Poo!" I grinned. "Only trouble is, there's no way of getting inside the bag to taste the P.L.O.P."

Perhaps Flo would be small enough...

"OUCH!" she yelped, as I tried to shove her through the tiny gap in the knot. But even she was too big.

"Now we'll never reach that P.L.O.P!" I sighed.

"My antennae hurt!" groaned Flo.

"Shhh!" I hissed. I could just make out a human voice beside the bin.

It was a woman talking. "He did a tiny poo – hardly worth the bother!" she said. "He's bound to go again."

I couldn't believe what I was hearing. The dog would need to poo again? There would be another P.L.O.P!

"Quick!" I cried. "Let's go!"

"But I want more muffin," said Flo, flying back to the bottom of the coffee cup.

JACK SPLAT

"I don't know what's the matter with him," the woman went on in a muffled voice. "He ate a pair of my old socks last night. Imagine that!"

"Old socks!" I cried, speeding towards the top of the bin. "What did I tell you, Flo? My sense of smell is never wrong!"

"I said it was socks," said Flo, between mouthfuls of muffin.

"Shhh! Just keep quiet and follow me!" I ordered.

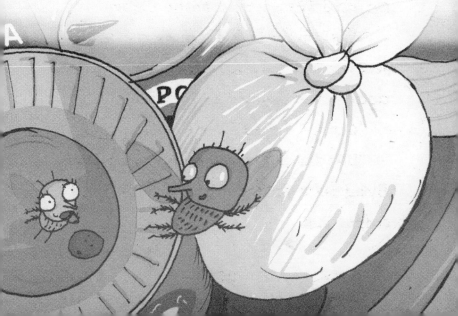

"But—"

"Come on! All we have to do is follow that dog until he does his business again."

"Which dog?" asked Flo, buzzing to the top of the bin at last.

"The dog who did the P.L.O.P., of course!" I snapped. "Why are girls so stu— Ah, I see!"

As I peered out of the bin, I saw there were three dogs standing below us. Three possible poopers!

"How will we ever know which one it was?" cried Flo.

D–F

D is for Dog Poo, of course! If it isn't poop scooped, a single dog plop can take over a year to disappear. Yum! That's like opening a street café for flies.

E is for Elephant Poo – you've got to think big! Some companies recycle ellie poop to make paper gifts and flowers. Think how romantic that would be on Valentine's Day!

FOR MY SWEETHEART, THINKING OF ~~YOU~~ POO!

Roses are red, violets are blue
I've bought you a flower made out of poo!

F is for Farts. You humans make some perfect stinkers! Most of you fart enough to fill a small balloon each day.

FABULOUS FART FACTS

1. You're most likely to fart early in the morning. If you're polite and try to hold them in, these guffs will escape while you're asleep at night.

2. As gas pops out, your bum vibrates. This causes the sound of the fart.

3. People who swallow lots of air fart more than people who don't. Try chewing meals with your mouth shut if you don't want to parp a tune in your trousers!

Bonus Fact: Even fish fart! Look out for botty-bubbles in your goldfish bowl!

Chapter Three
A Tale of Three Tails

I circled low over the bin, waving my antennae to try and get a good sniff of the three mutts beneath me. There was a huge hairy one (let's call him Frizzle). A stumpy one that looked like a sausage on legs (he's Sizzle). And a mean looking one, with drool dripping from his chops (he can be Dribble).

"This is all your fault, Flo! Now I have no idea which owner I heard talking!" I thundered. "If you hadn't gone back to that mouldy muffin, I'd have flown straight out of the bin."

JACK SPLAT

"But you're so clever, Jack," said Flo. "I'm sure you'll work out which dog did the P.L.O.P!"

"Of course I will!" I said. "It just might take a couple of minutes, that's all... The first thing is to work out which mutt belongs with which human."

At least that wasn't too tricky. Go on, Buddy. Give it a try.

Yikes! I didn't like the look of the old lady. I've got to tell you, grannies have always given me the creeps, ever since I was a maggot and my mum used to sing us this horrible song.

Oh no!

Suddenly, Flo started singing the exact same song:

♪ **"There was an old lady who** ♫ **swallowed a—"**

"Please don't sing that song!" I cried desperately.

"Why not?" said Flo. "Mum used to sing it to us when we were maggots. It was one of my favourites!"

Over by the bench, Grandma Guzzle-Gums was rummaging through her handbag, popping sweets into her mouth. Little black liquorice sweets, which looked exactly like flies! Every time she chewed, I imagined it was me she was eating!

But Flo kept singing as if it were all a big joke.

♪ **"I don't know why she swallowed a—"**

"I CAN'T THINK IF YOU'RE SINGING!" I bellowed. "I ... er ... I need to listen out for vital clues! That's super-important in an investigation, Flo!"

Perched on the top of the bin, I strained my antennae, trying to hear what the owners were saying without having to get any closer to Grandma. But they were only droning on about the "lovely hot weather we're having".

JACK SPLAT

Nothing useful. Like which of their dogs had plopped the perfect poo! I still couldn't recognize the voice I'd heard either – it had sounded all echoey inside the bin.

I twitched my antennae towards the dogs. Perhaps they were saying something useful...

Not likely!

"NICE DAY FOR WALKIES!" woofed Frizzle, as they all sniffed each other's bums.

"NICE DAY!" barked Dribble.

"FOR WALKIES!" yapped Sizzle.

"So which one is *the plopper?*" asked Flo, staring up at me expectantly.

"Shhh!" I said. "I need ABSOLUTE calm and ABSOLUTE quiet."

"ABSOLUTE calm and ABSOLUTE quiet," repeated Flo.

"Like any great fly detective," I told her, "I need to weigh up the evidence."

"...Weigh up the evidence."

"And examine the facts."

"...Examine the facts."

"Will you stop repeating everything I say!" I snapped.

"Stop repeating... Sorry!" said Flo.

"Then – and only then – can I name my suspect." I waved my antennae in the air, sniffing for suspicious pongs. "In this case, we're searching for the dog that did the P.L.O.P. We must wait and watch ... and he will strike again! I'm a fly detective like Inspector Pooseau," I told Flo. "The famous French fly detective who solved the mystery of 'The Pink Pooper'. All I need is one tiny clue."

"A clue to find the poo?" asked Flo.

"Yes. And stop staring at me. I can't think straight."

"Sorry!" Flo turned her back.

"Flo?"

"Yes, Jack."

"You're still staring at me. You're a fly. Your eyes can see out of the back of your head."

"Sorry, Jack!"

She hopped away across the top of the bin.

"Imagine I'm *the genius detective* Flylock Holmes," I called after her. "I do the thinking and have the clever ideas. You can be my assistant, Dr Swatson!"

Flylock Holmes
and
Dr Swatson

The World Flymous Sleuth, and his trusty assistant – following the clues that lead to poos.

"But Jack—"

"Assistants don't talk, Flo! They wait until they are given instructions."

"But Jack?"

"What is it, Flo?"

"The dogs are leaving. Look!"

"Right! I was ... er ... expecting that!" I said. I shot up into the sky to get an aerial view of the situation.

JACK SPLAT

The *three mutts* were all going in different directions. Frizzle was bounding towards the playground, as his owner followed with her buggy.

Dribble and his sweaty owner set off at a jog towards the Woodland Walk.

And Sizzle was trotting to the rose garden with the little old lady.

"Well, we don't want to go to the rose garden!" I said. "Nothing but stinky flowers and boring bumblebees!" The truth was, I didn't want to go anywhere near that guzzly old grandma unless I absolutely had to.

"But look!" whined Flo. "The old lady's got a ball of wool poking out of her bag! That's our first clue!"

"Yikes! And spiky knitting needles, too!" I shuddered.

JACK SPLAT

Flo clapped her wings together. "I bet she's knitting a new pair of woolly socks because the dog ate her old ones!"

"That's a rubbish clue!" I said. "Old ladies knit all the time. Everyone knows that!"

"But—"

"We don't have time to argue. The dogs are getting away. Look!"

"All right," sulked Flo.

"Forget about knitting needles!" I said. "I'm Flylock Holmes! The important clue is that the dog's owner was surprised the P.L.O.P. was so small. A big dog = a big poo! It's elementary, my dear Swatson!"

Before Flo could argue, I took off at top speed and followed Frizzle's huge, hairy bum across the park.

"You'd expect a BIG poo from something that size!" I said.

MY ENCYCLO**POO**DIA™
G–I

 G is for Gas! The chemical make-up of fart gas depends on: a) What you eat. b) How long you hold the fart in. c) What kind of germs you have living in your gut. Someone should collect rare farts in jam jars, then open a Gallery of Guffs for everyone to admire!

 H is for Hyena Poo. Hyenas live on the half-chewed remains of dead animals, which hunters like lions have killed. Sometimes their poo comes out bright white because they've eaten so many bones!

 I is for Iguana Poop – these big lizards have surprisingly pretty poo. Their plops look like twisted rope! I'm not a fussy eater, but good presentation is always nice.

Chapter Four
A Hairy Situation

"Keep up!" I cried, as Flo flapped along as slowly as a butterfly. "The real Flylock Holmes would never have found the famous Hound of the Baskerville's poop if *his* Dr Swatson had been as slow as you are!"

"But my wings hurt," moaned Flo, as the big hairy dog bounded across the park, stopping every now and again to chase his own tail.

"WHERE'S MY TAIL? WHERE'S MY TAIL?" he barked in a BIG, DEEP voice.

"It's behind you!" I said. But, of

course, dogs never listen to us flies. They don't understand a word we say.

I got as close to his rear end as I could. "One guff and we'll know if this is our pooper!" I told Flo, as she caught up at last.

"You're so clever, Flylock!" she said.

"Who him? Clever?!" said a sneering voice. "He's just a dumb housefly, kid!"

I glanced over as a HUGE bluebottle flew up alongside us. Oh no! I knew this fly. I'd met him hanging round a picnic here last week.

"Hi, Baz," I groaned. He's the biggest know-all I've ever met. And he treats me like a tiny gnat, teasing me and bossing me about, just because he's twice my size and has a fat, shiny bum.

"Jack's idea of clever is to fly into a glass of juice and drown!" Baz laughed.

"As if!" I said. (OK, I did have a close shave with some apple juice at the picnic, but I came to my senses in time.)

"Aren't you going to introduce me to your little girlfriend?" said Baz, as we landed on a lamp post, and watched Frizzle run round and round it, chasing his tail.

Girlfriend? YUCK! "Flo's not my girlfriend!" I snapped. "She's my cousin. I'm just looking after her, that's all."

"Like Nanny McFly, or Mary Ploppins!" Baz snorted.

JACK SPLAT

"I'm not a soppy nanny!" I said.
"I'm only babysitting for today!"

"Having fun?" Baz sniggered.

"We're just ... flying about," I said,
shrugging my antennae. There was no
way I was going to tell Baz about
the great P.L.O.P. hunt.

"There's not much going on here,"
I said. "If I were you, I'd check out the
nappy bins by the sandpit. I've heard
they haven't been emptied for days."

"Really?" said Baz. I reckon he'd
have gone too, if it hadn't been for Flo
and her big proboscis.

"Jack's just made up this brilliant
game," she said. "He's Flylock Holmes
and I'm Dr Swatson..."

"A game!" Baz was off again,
laughing so hard I thought he was

going to slip off the lamp post. "You're like a couple of baby maggots!"

"It's NOT a game," I said. "It's serious detective business!"

"Oh! Serious detective business!" Now Baz laughed so hard he did fall off.

SPLAT! He landed flat on his back on the grass, his legs waving in the air.

"Quick, Flo!" I hissed, as Baz staggered to his feet. "Let's go!" I dived towards the thick, fluffy fur on Frizzle's bum. "We can hide in here until that big bully Baz has gone."

Frizzle was massive and his hair was so thick I don't think he even felt us land.

"Baz will never find us now!" I grinned, as we wound our way deep into the dog's matted fur.

"And if we stick around here, we'll be the first to know if Frizzle does a poo!" I added. "Sometimes I amaze myself, I'm so brilliant. Look! There are even some snacks for the journey."

Frizzle's fur was full of bits of old food. I was just heading towards a nice lump of scrambled egg when...

"Watch out, Flo! He's sitting down!"

THUD!

"Ouch!" I yelped, straightening out my crumpled wing. "We were lucky not to be squashed alive."

"Where next, Cousin Jack?" said Flo shakily.

"Follow me!" We scrambled higher

and higher through the deep fur on Frizzle's back.

"What's he doing now?" cried Flo. We clung on for dear life as Frizzle started shaking from side to side, like a hairy washing machine on fast spin.

"I think he's having a **SCRATCH!**" I cried, as I was thrown sideways.

I tried to escape through the jungle of hair, but his fur was so matted I couldn't even flap my wings and fly out.

The **SCRATCHING** stopped for a second.

"Is it over?" squealed Flo.

"No! Our troubles are only just beginning," I warned. "When a dog **SCRATCHES** it means he has—"

"Hello!" said a chirpy voice to our left.

JACK SPLAT

"Hello!" said a chirpy voice to our right.

"Fleas!" I groaned.

"Yes, fleas!" said both the chirpy voices at once. Two jumpy grey insects appeared beside us.

"I'm Fleedle-dum!" The first grinned.

"And I'm Fleedle-dee!" cried the second.

"No, *I'm* Fleedle-dee," snapped the first. "You're Fleedle-d—"

"Listen! You don't happen to know if this dog did a poo earlier, do you?" I said.

But it was no use. The fleas weren't listening to me. They jumped up and down, shouting and trying to bite each other, but they kept missing and taking bites out of the dog instead.

"I'm Fleedle-dum!"

Chomp!

Chomp!

"No, I'm Fleedle-dum!"

Chomp!

"You're Fleedle-dee!"

Chomp!

"No, you're Fleedle-dee."

Chomp!

Chomp!

And every time they bit him, Frizzle **SCRATCHED** harder. Flo and I were thrown around like a couple of grasshoppers on a trampoline.

"I feel dog sick!" groaned Flo.

She'd turned as green as a pot of

mushy peas in a chip shop bin. "Come on!" I coaxed. "Dogs scratch with their back legs. If we head towards the front end, we won't wobble so much."

"Are we nearly there yet?" groaned Flo, as we crawled on up towards the dog's nose.

"No. Anyway, this is all your fault," I reminded her. "If you hadn't tried to make friends with Baz, we wouldn't have needed to hide and—"

"I'm bored!" moaned Flo. "Let's sing!"

"There was an old lady who swallowed a—"

"How about we play Fly Spy?" I butted in. "Fly spy with my little eye something beginning with 'F'!" Anything to stop Flo singing that HORRIBLE song. At least Frizzle wasn't

SCRATCHING and shaking much now.

"'F' for fur?" said Flo.

"No."

"Fleas?"

"No! Can't see them any more, thank goodness."

"Fart!"

"Farts are invisible, Flo!"

It was going to be a long day...

On we crawled, occasionally glimpsing flashes of green grass in the park beyond.

"France?"

It was only the hope of that perfect plop that kept me sane.

"Fresh air!"

"No, Flo! You can't see fresh air!"

"Yes you can," she said. "Look!"

She was right! We were out of

Frizzle's fur at last and balanced on the tip of his nose. He'd taken us right to the other side of the park, beside the ice-cream van. His frizzy-haired owner joined the queue with her buggy.

"Can we have an ice cream, too?" said Flo.

"No! We have to stay focused on our mission. We have to..."

Just then, Frizzle's nose started twitching beneath my feet.

BURP!

The stale smell of old dog food drifted towards us.

Dog food... Oh no! We were following a false lead.

"This isn't our suspect," I sighed. "His burp would smell of sardines and sausage and stinky socks if that's what he'd eaten," I groaned. "We'd be barking mad to ignore the evidence. Frizzle did not make the P.L.O.P!"

But Flo didn't seem to care. "I want an ice cream!" she moaned.

MY ENCYCLOPOODIA™
J–M

J is for Jellyfish Poo. Jellyfish don't have bums ... so they poop out of their mouths!

K is for Kangaroo Poo. Question: where does a baby kangaroo poo when it's in its mother's pouch? Nice!

L is for Loo Paper – personally, I don't see the point, but you humans use about 83 million rolls of the stuff each day!

M is for Meerkat Poop. Watch out, though. Those guys eat scorpions, so their poo could have a sting in its tail!

Chapter Five

Swat's Up?

"I want to try vanilla," said Flo, "and strawberry ... and chocolate!"

She leaped off the end of Frizzle's nose and headed for the ice-cream van.

"How can you even think about ice cream at a time like this?" I said. "We have to look for the next dog."

"Please!" begged Flo, as Frizzle's curly-haired owner pushed her buggy up to the window of the van. "Mum told me about ice cream when I was a maggot, but I've never tried it for myself!" Flo turned her big fly eyes on me and my heart melted like a lolly in the sun.

"You've never tried ice cream?"
I couldn't believe it! "All right. Just one
slurp and then we're back on the poo
trail." There was no sign of the other
two dogs anyway. And no sign of Baz
either. My cunning trick of hiding in
Frizzle's hair must have worked.

"You're the best!"
Flo tried to give me
a soppy kiss with
her proboscis.

"Ew! Get off me!" I cried,
darting out of the way.

We landed on the handle of Mrs
Frizz-Head's buggy as she tied
Frizzle to the railings and trundled
into the playground. Inside the buggy,
Baby-Frizz was already dribbling

delicious looking rivers of spit and ice
cream down his chin.

"Just be careful!" I said, as Flo
and I crawled over the buggy's
sunshade, ready to dive into the ice
cream below. "Mothers can be
dangerous! I've fought them before."

Flo, as usual, paid no attention.
"The ice cream looks so runny and
creamy and— YIKES!"

Sure enough, Mrs Frizz-Head
spotted us. She grabbed a packet
of baby wipes out of the buggy and
smacked it down on the sunshade.
THWACK! She just missed Flo by a
wing-tip.

THWACK! She was aiming for me now.

She didn't stand a chance, of
course. I was in the sky before the

JACK SPLAT

packet even hit the buggy. The number of times you humans try to swat me is hilarious. You always go about it in the wrong way. Seeing as we're pals, Buddy, I'll share a few tips:

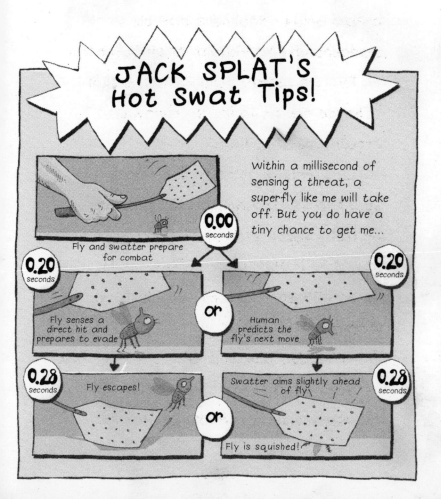

JACK SPLAT'S Hot Swat Tips!

0.00 seconds

Within a millisecond of sensing a threat, a superfly like me will take off. But you do have a tiny chance to get me...

Fly and swatter prepare for combat

0.20 seconds — Fly senses a direct hit and prepares to evade

or

0.20 seconds — Human predicts the fly's next move

0.28 seconds — Fly escapes!

or

Swatter aims slightly ahead of fly — **0.28 seconds**

Fly is squished!

"Shoo! Dirty little things!" Mrs Frizz-Head cried, waving the baby wipes hopelessly in the air as Flo and I scooted sideways.

Baby-Frizz peered out of his buggy to see what she was shouting about.

THWACK! Mrs Frizz-Head missed us, but smacked his ice cream right out of his hand. SPLAT!

"Waaaaaaaaaa!" Baby-Frizz began to wail.

"What are you waiting for, Flo? A party invite?" I cried, bombing towards the spilt ice cream. "Human mothers never let their kids eat anything off the ground. It's weird, I know, but that's the way they are!"

Sure enough, Mrs Frizz-Head wheeled her screaming child back to the van.

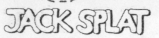

"I'll get you a new ice cream, darling," she said. "That one is dirty!"

"It's freezing," shivered Flo, as we sunk up to our knees in ice cream.

I froze too. But not because I was cold.

"Do you hear that?" I said.

A low, menacing hum filled the air. **Vrooooooooooooooooooooooooooooom.**

"What is it?" squeaked Flo.

Before I could answer, three wasps appeared in the sky. As they dived towards us, I could see their black and gold stripes glinting in the sun.

"They're after the ice cream!" I yelled. "Let's go!"

"I've only had one slurp!"

"Just do as you're told!" I shouted.

But it was too late. The wasps swooped down at us in perfect formation.

"Just don't make them angry," I whispered. "They're fine if you don't get on the wrong side of them."

I didn't want to worry Flo, but I've heard if you upset these guys, they can paralyze a fly with one sting!

"Hey! Cool landing!" I waved a leg as the wasps paddled through the melting ice cream towards us.

"Move along, flies!" roared the biggest wasp. "Vanilla Mountain is under the control of the Wasp Airforce.

Civilian insects are ordered to leave the area."

"I'm not a civilian!" said Flo. "I'm a girl!"

"Are you disobeying an order?" barked the Wasp Commander.

"No, sir!" I hopped in front of Flo. "Come on, Flo. We were leaving anyway."

I started to edge away. They were welcome to Vanilla Mountain. All I wanted to do was get out of here and find the P.L.O.P.

"But it's *our* ice cream!" cried Flo. "We found it first, you big, stripy bullies!"

"I thought we weren't going to make them angry," I hissed. "Remember?"

I was shaking like a daddy-long-legs in the wind. You know me, Buddy — fearless Jack Splat! I'm afraid of nothing and no one (well, no one except old ladies). But have you ever looked closely at a wasp's bum?

Wasp's bum

With this needle-like sting a wasp can squeeze poisonous venom out through its bum and inject its helpless victim. Scary, huh?

"We need to teach these flies a lesson," said the Wasp Commander.

"Don't worry, we're going," I said, as the smaller wasps moved closer.

"I'm not scared of you! Pin-bums!" cried Flo.

I've got to hand it to her, Flo really knows how to make a bad situation worse!

JACK SPLAT

"ATTACK!" roared the Commander.

The wasps shot forward, ready to sting.

Vroooooooooooooooooooooooooooom!

Ahhhhhhhhhhhhhhhhhhhhhhhhhhhhhhhhh!

"Quick, Flo!" I yelped. "Let's get out of here!"

MY ENCYCLO**POO**DIA™
N–P

 N is for Nappies – the perfect place to store poo!

 O is for Owl Puke. (OK – so it's not poo – it comes out the other end. But it is very tasty.) Owls sick up pellets full of all the little mousey-bones, fur and tails that their stomachs can't digest. I love leftovers!

 P is for Penguin Poo. You eat it frozen, like fish-flavour ice cream. Yum!

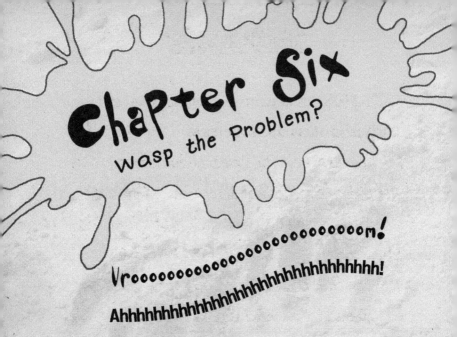

Chapter Six
Wasp the Problem?

Vrooooooooooooooooooooooooom!

Ahhhhhhhhhhhhhhhhhhhhhhhhhhhh!

Flo and I zoomed across the
playground with the wasps, like stripy
fighter jets, hot on our tail.

We flew down the slide, wove
through the swings, zoomed low over
the sandpit, dodged a gang of big kids
playing tag and swooped up the
climbing frame.

"Keep up, Flo! The wasps are
gaining on us!" Normally a superfly
like me can out-swoop anybody, but

with slowcoach Flo flapping like a ladybird it was hopeless.

"I know how to lose these stripy pests! We need to distract them with something sweet! Head for the ice-cream van," I called. "Mrs Frizz-Head's bought an ice lolly this time!"

"Goodie!" cried Flo. "Is it orange flavour?"

"It's not for us!" I said, heading straight for Mrs Frizz-Head. "Now for once in your life, follow me and do EXACTLY what I do."

We flashed by so fast, I don't think Mrs Frizz-Head saw us. But she did see the wasps... And they saw the lovely drippy lolly!

"Food target due north!" bellowed the Commander.

JACK SPLAT

"Shoo!" cried Mrs Frizz-Head, waving her arms in the air.

"Wasp the matter with her?" I laughed, as Flo and I flew on to the roof of the van to watch. "She shouldn't make them angry!"

"ATTACK!" barked the Commander. Mrs Frizz-Head tried to beat the wasps away, but she was waving so wildly, she dropped the lolly.

"WAAHHHH!" wailed Baby-Frizz, as the wasps dive-bombed towards their bright orange target.

The second the wasps landed, their feet froze to the lolly.

"Looking cool, guys!" I smirked.

"RETREAT!" ordered the Commander.

The wasps tried to take off, but their feet were stuck fast.

Then Mrs Frizz-Head grabbed
the end of the lolly stick and
tossed the whole thing – wasps
and all – into a litter bin.

"Come on, Flo. They'll be
out of there soon. They
just need a little time to
cool down!" I sniggered.
"Meanwhile, we've got a
poo to look for."

"You were totally
fly-tastic!" cheered Flo,
as we set off.

"It's all in a day's work
for a superfly!" I grinned.
"Let's head for the Woodland
Walk and look for Dribble.
We've got clues to find,
Dr Swatson!"

"Lead on, Flylock!" cheered Flo. I was almost glad she was tagging along. Then she had to go and spoil it.

"But I want to go to the rose garden first and look for the old lady's dog. I'm still sure he's the one who ate the socks."

"Well, I'm Flylock Holmes and I say—"

"You're scared of that little old lady, aren't you?" Flo beamed.

"Don't be ridiculous! Why would I...?"

But Flo was already heading in the direction of the garden. She was singing at the top of her voice as she buzzed past the nappy bins.

♫ **"There was an old lady who swallowed a—"** ♫

"Please stop singing! Just pipe down!" I said. "This is where I told Baz to go. I don't want him to hear us!"

"If it isn't Nanny McFly!" sneered a familiar voice, as the bluebottle flew out of the bin.

"Thanks a lot, Flo!"

"You two are so sweet!" Baz chuckled, buzzing over. "Are you still playing your little detective game?"

"No!" I said quickly.

"Yes!" said Flo. "We're hunting for the perfect poo!"

"Thanks, cousin!" I sighed. "Why don't you tell him ALL our secrets?"

"OK!" Flo giggled. "Jack is scared of little old—"

"I didn't *mean* tell him our secrets," I hissed. "I was being sarcastic!"

By now we'd reached the edge of the rose garden and Baz showed no sign of buzzing off. I glanced nervously around, looking for the old lady. Luckily, there was no sign of her.

"We can come back and search for Sizzle later," I whispered to Flo. "First, let's find Dribble. I'm sure his owner is running round the Woodland Walk."

"No she's not!" cried Flo. "Look, Dribble is right there!"

Sure enough, the slobbery dog and his sweaty owner were jogging right past the rose garden.

"Actually, I knew they'd come this way," I said. "That's why I came over here in the first place."

"No you didn't!" said Flo. "You wanted to—"

"Stop talking!" I hissed. "We've got plop secret clues to follow!"

"Yeah right!" Baz laughed, sticking in his antennae where they weren't wanted. "Call yourself a detective? You couldn't find a dog poo at a puppy show! You're clueless — or pooless!"

"I'll show you!" I cried. Baz might think I'm nothing but a soppy nanny, but I'd prove him wrong. "I'm Jack Splat — Number One Poop Snoop!" I said. "My investigations have already proved Frizzle wasn't the pooper. Now it's time to follow that trail of drool!"

"I'm coming too," said Baz. "If there's going to be poo, I want first dibs!"

JACK SPLAT

"Fine!" I flapped my wings at top speed as Dribble and his owner sprinted away. "If you can keep up!"

Baz might be proud of his big, shiny bum, but it weighs him down. Even Flo was flying faster than him.

"Wait!" I warned, as she shot past me too, heading straight for the dog's dribbling mouth.

"I'm going to sniff his breath!" she called back. "It's a clue, Flylock! I'll see what he's been eating."

"Careful, Flo," I warned. "Look out for his—"

CHOMP!

"—teeth!"

It was too late. Dribble had snapped her up in his big, sticky jaws!

MY ENCYCLOPOODIA™
Q–S

 Q is for Queen Bee Poop. Her poop, like any bee's, is runny and yellow. Better hope the bee-keeper doesn't get confused when he's putting honey in a jar!

 R is for Roach Poo. If there's not much food about, a baby cockroach can live on nothing but its parents' poop. Clever creatures, cockroaches!

 S is for Snow Leopard Poo. These big cats are so rare, that to find them in the wild, scientists have to borrow poop from zoos to teach their tracker dogs the smell.

Chapter Seven
Bubble Trouble

"Spit my cousin out!" I called desperately, zooming after Dribble.

I could just make out Flo's faint voice, as I dived low over his muzzle.

"It's so dark in here! I can't see the way out!" whimpered Flo. "Help!"

"Don't worry! I'll save you," I shouted, as Dribble stopped in the middle of the path while his owner stretched and touched her toes.

The dog shook his head from side to side. Sploshes of drool flew in every direction.

JACK SPLAT

"Please open your
mouth!" I begged, landing on
Dribble's ear. But, of course,
he ignored me.

"Some nanny you are!" said
Baz. "You can't even look after
one tiny little flylet!"

"Buzz off!" I said. "You're
not helping!"

"Fine!" Baz hopped on to the
dog's back, but stayed watching me.

"Nice doggy!" I whispered, as I
crawled down on to his nose. Streams
of dribble tumbled like a waterfall
from his chops. If I could just get
under one of his lips, I could peek inside
his mouth and help Flo escape.

But Mrs Sweaty, his owner, stopped
stretching and sped off down the path.

Dribble ran
after her.
I clung on as
tight as I could
to the outside of his
pink rubbery jowls, keeping well
out of the way of his ENORMOUS
sharp teeth.

"Don't worry, Flo! Cousin Jack is
here!" I called.

"Yeah! And what's your plan?"
asked Baz.

"My plan? My plan is to..." I had to
think of something fast. Flo might be a
little pest, but I couldn't abandon her.

Suddenly, I was hurled sideways as
Dribble turned and bounded across the
grass. He was heading straight for
the pond.

JACK SPLAT

Baz shot off the dog's back and into a tree. "I'm not going to get wet!"

"DUCKS! DUCKS!" Dribble barked.

The birds flapped into the middle of the pond.

"DUCKS! DUCKS!"

This was my big chance. "Flo!" I cried, sticking my head inside Dribble's jagged jaws. I weaved sideways, dodging his deadly teeth each time he opened his mouth to bark.

"Flo! Fly towards me! You've got to get out while he's barking."

"Jack!" cried Flo. She shot out from Dribble's jaws in a ball of spit.

JACK SPLAT

"It was so dark in there. Then I heard your voice. You saved me!"

"It was nothing!" I grinned, crawling on to Dribble's snout. "It was easy for a superfly like—"

"Look out, Jack!"

Splosh!

Dribble bounded right into the pond, taking me with him.

As the dog plunged into the water, I was washed clean off the end of his nose. Down, down, down I sank through the freezing, muddy water. My body felt heavy ... too cold to move. I knew if I wanted to get out of here, I was going to have to fight with all my fly powers.

"I will NOT drown!" I told myself, kicking all of my six legs as hard as I could. "I am a superfly!"

I bobbed up to the surface like a bubble in a glass of coke. POP!

"There you are!" cried Flo, skimming above the water. "Poor Jack! You look so wet!"

I scrambled on to a lily pad, puking up pond water from my proboscis.

"I *am* wet!" I spluttered.

"You showed me the way out of Dribble's mouth!" said Flo. "You're a real hero!"

"Like James Pond, Bubble-O-Seven!" Baz laughed, coming up beside her.

Flo giggled.

"I don't know why I bothered," I gasped. "If you hadn't been so stupid—"

JACK SPLAT

"Jack!"

"And now we'll probably lose the dog, too. Look, he's swimming back to the bank. And—"

"Jack!"

"I'm not listening, Flo—"

"Fine!" she snapped. "But you might want to know – there's a big fat frog RIGHT behind you."

YIKES!

"R-ribbit! Are you r-ready to be eaten?" said the frog, stickily.

In a split second, I was in the air – my wings just dry enough to lift me.

The frog's long tongue shot out, unrolling like flypaper.

It missed my back leg by a millimetre, as I swerved left.

"You can't catch me!" I whooped. "I'm Jack Splat – superfly!"

"Look out!" cried Flo. "You're falling!"

I flapped my wings desperately. But they were still soggy with pond water and I couldn't stay airborne.

I floated down like a falling leaf. Below me, the frog licked his lips with his mouth wide open.

"Goodbye, Flo," I cried. "This is it! I'm frog food!"

"Too r-right! Bye bye, Jack Splat... Hello, Jack Snack!" croaked the frog.

"FROG! FROG!"

Dribble bounded back into the pond, barking his head off.

"R-ribbit! You're r-really lucky that r-rotten dog showed up!" slurped the frog. And he dived into the water.

But I wasn't out of danger yet. Still flapping helplessly, I spiralled down towards the pond.

"FROG?" Dribble sploshed about beneath me, too stupid to realize the frog had swum away. Using my superfly radar senses, I aimed for the dog's tail above the water.

I flung myself sideways and just grabbed the tip.

"FROG?" Dribble barked again.

Crawling up his tail to safety, I watched as a trail of bubbles broke the water beneath me.

Parp!

"Dribble has farted!" I cried. "Quick, Flo! Sniff those bubbles! This could be a vital clue."

MY ENCYCLO**POO**DIA™
T–V

T is for Tiger Poo. In the Vietnam war, American secret agents disguised listening devices as tiger poo so that they could spy on people deep in the jungle. That's what I call plop secret!

U is for U-bend. The twist in the toilet pipe where most poo gets stuck.

V is for Vulture Poo. The acid in vulture droppings is so strong that it can be used to kill bacteria. I wish people would clean their kitchens with it. Vulture plop would be so much nicer than that disgusting lemon-scented spray!

Chapter Eight

Poo Good to be True

As I clung to Dribble's tail, excitement surged through me. My strength returned as I flicked my antennae above the water — hoping for the scent of sardines, sausage and stinky socks. Instead, there was a sweet pong of...

"Treacle pudding?" I groaned, as Dribble climbed out of the pond and shook himself dry.

"Oh no! He's not the plopper either!" I cried, as I was thrown through the air in a wave of wet dog hair and spray towards a nearby tree.

JACK SPLAT

I landed *SPLAT* on a leaf.

"I could have told you that ages ago," said Flo, as she and Baz flew over. "Didn't you smell his drool? It was all sweet and sticky. No socks or sausage or sardines!"

"Well, excuse me!" I said. "When I was clinging to his jaws, covered in slobber, I was thinking of other things. Like saving you! Not how nice his dribble might taste with a splash of custard..."

Baz giggled.

My antennae were about to explode I was so furious. Flo was turning into a right little know-it-all! Baz was definitely a bad influence.

Just then, the air was filled with a familiar smell... LIQUORICE!

JACK SPLAT

Yikes! I looked down through the branches of the tree, to see the old lady and Sizzle pass right beneath us. They were shuffling towards the pond with a bag of stale bread.

JACK SPLAT

As she bumbled along, old Grandma
Guzzle-Gums was still popping those
black liquorice sweets into her mouth.

My legs started to tremble so hard
that the leaf we were standing on
began to wobble.

"Why are you shaking like a soppy
dragonfly?" Baz sneered. "It's not
that little pooch down there, is it?
Is Fearless Flylock scared of sausage
dogs?"

"No, I am not!"

"But he *is* scared of old ladies!" Flo
giggled. And she started to sing.

🎵 **"There was an old lady who** 🎵
swallowed a—" 🎵

"I know that song!" whooped Baz.
"My mum used to sing it when I was a
maggot."

And he joined in too.

♫ **"I don't know why she swallowed a—"** ♫

This was the stuff of nightmares! "Please BE QUIET!" I begged. But, of course, they ignored me.

There was only one way to shut them up. One terrible, horrible, unthinkable way...

"I am not scared!" I snapped. "And I'll prove it." I flew a tiny little way down the branch, edging ever so slightly closer to Grandma Guzzle-Gums. The liquorice tang of her sweets caught in my antennae.

It was horrible! But there was NO WAY I was going to let Baz see I was afraid.

"This dog is our last suspect,"

I said coolly. "Our only remaining chance to find the P.L.O.P!"

"DUCKS! DUCKS!" yapped Sizzle, as Grandma threw chunks of bread into the water.

"I bet you wouldn't be brave enough to land on Grandma's nose!" said Baz.

"Y-yes I would!" I said. "J-just you watch me!"

What was I saying? I'd rather swallow fly spray! I'd rather dance with a black widow spider. I'd rather...

"Get on with it then!" urged Baz.

I took off, my wings trembling.

"What I need is a plan!" I muttered. "An 'avoid Grandma's nose' plan..."

I was only six wing beats away from her face, when I had a totally brilliant idea. BET BAZ BACK! That big show-off would never refuse a dare!

"I bet you wouldn't land on her chin, Baz," I said, doing a casual loop the loop back towards him.

"I would!" He was off like a shot. Job done! Now Grandma would eat him and we could all go home happy!

"Careful, Baz!" cried Flo.

He dived past the old lady's chomping jaws. "Why, Grandma, what BIG teeth you've got!" He laughed.

If I had eyelids I'd have closed them. If I didn't have super 360 degree, all-round vision, I'd have looked away. But I couldn't. Even though I'd dared him to do it, I stared in horror as Baz landed right on Grandma's wrinkly chin.

"Shoo!" The old lady flapped her arms.

"Ha! Bet she swallows him!" I said to Flo, trying to sound calm. "That song is no joke, you know!"

"See?" said Baz. He was hovering in mid-air now, right in front of her jaws. "I'm not scared!"

Then...

CHOMP!

In one quick gulp, old Grandma Guzzle-Gums popped another liquorice sweet into her mouth and ... gulp! ... Baz went in with it!

"Baz!" cried Flo. "Do something, Jack! Save him!"

"Me? Why would I want to help a big show-off like Baz?"

But I knew she was right. I couldn't

just hover about and watch that
gummy old monster swallow Baz whole.

"OK — I have a plan," I cried. "It's
madness, but it's the only thing we can
do. You need to land on her face, Flo!
It's like when Dribble barked at the
ducks. We've got to get her to open her
mouth. Wriggle and jiggle and tickle
her. Do some of your crazy ballet!"

Flo swooped on to Grandma's chin,
twirling and swirling and dancing about.

Meanwhile, with super-cool daring, I
rested right under her nose, just above
her top lip.

"I can't believe I'm doing this!" I
shuddered. I could see the little grey
hairs twitching in Grandma's nostrils,
her face was covered in wrinkles as
deep as a Venus Flytrap and ...

worst of all ... I could smell her foul,
fly-gobbling breath. Yikes!

"Go for it, Flo!" I roared and I
aimed at Grandma's nose with my
best fly-football kick.

Grandma's face twitched
and she waved her arms
about. "Shoo! Stop it!
That tickles!" The
moment she opened her
mouth, Baz shot out
from between her
gums, covered in sticky
liquorice spit.

"T-thanks!" he stammered, as we
all flew back to our tree. "I didn't
expect you to save me, Jack."

"I didn't do it for you!" I chuckled. "I
did it for the little old lady. I wouldn't

have liked her to swallow a fly! We're covered in germs. She might have died!"

Baz shook his wings, looking cross. Then he burst out laughing, sending a big blob of liquorice slobber flying from the end of his proboscis.

"You're the best, Jack!" said Flo.

"Thanks!" I grinned. "And talking of germs ... can you guys smell that?"

"I can't smell anything except liquorice!" said Baz.

"No! Not liquorice," I said, as the unmistakable pong of poo filled the air. "Sniff that. That's not just any poo..." There was a whiff of socks and sausage and sardines...

"The P.L.O.P!" I cheered, as beneath the tree, Sizzle left an ENORMOUS, woolly pile of poop!

"I told you it was him all along!" cried Flo. "I knew he'd eaten the socks."

"Well ... er ... it's important for a detective to follow all the clues in the proper order," I said. "Right through to the very end."

"To the rear end!" Flo giggled.

"Exactly!" I grinned. "Now STOP TALKING AND COME ON!"

Flo and I dived for the P.L.O.P. at exactly the same moment.

BAM! Our heads crashed together. And we landed head first – SPLAT – in the steaming pile.

"That was all your fault, Flo!" I laughed as we both tucked in. It really was the PERFECT LUMP OF POO! Better still, short-sighted Grandma hadn't noticed it under the tree. She wandered away without clearing up. Perhaps old ladies aren't so bad after all!

"Poor thing!" said Flo. "She'll be waiting all day for him to do another poo!"

"We should lend her a pair of antennae to sniff it out with!" I sniggered.

As I watched Grandma go, I saw that Baz was hanging back in the branches.

"Come on, Big Guy!" I called. "You've earned your share! There's plenty here for all three of us!"

He swooped down and join

"Yum! This really is the poofec

he slurped.

We seemed to have been guzzling for hours, when I heard a familiar voice.

"Jack? Is that you? And Flo, too? I knew you'd be in the park somewhere."

Aunt Emmeline landed beside us.

"Move over a bit!" she said, wiggling her bum. "This poo will make the perfect place to lay a new batch of eggs!"

I froze.

"You're going to lay more eggs?" I said. "Here? Now?"

"Of course," said Aunt Emmeline. "What better place to raise a family than in this splendid pile of poop?"

"Think of it, Jack," cried Flo. "There'll be hundreds of babies to look after. All exactly like me!"

Hundreds of babies? Exactly like Flo?

"I've got to go!" I said. "You enjoy the rest of the poo! Baz will help babysit ... he's brilliant with kids!"

Before any of them could argue, I shot into the sky like a rocket.

After all, I am NOT a nanny. I am

JACK SPLAT

Jack Splat – the superfly. I've got places to go ... clues to follow ... adventures to find.

"I'll miss you," called Flo, as I flew away across the park. "Don't forget to visit!"

"Goodbye," I called. And I knew I'd miss her too ... a teeny tiny flea's kneecap of a bit. But I wasn't going to act like a soppy butterfly and tell her that!

MY ENCYCLO**POODIA**™
W–Z

W is for Whale Poo. Blue Whales come to the surface to poo. Their enormous plops bob about on top of the ocean like a floater in the loo!

X is for eXtra Poo. I never say no to second helpings!

Y is for is for Yak Poo. People who live near Mount Everest burn yak doo-doo on their fires to keep warm. What a waste!

Z is for All The Poo in the Zoo! A visit to the zoo is like the biggest fly-buffet in the world. There's elephant poo, monkeys' business, hippo plops and camel doings. Yum!

Perhaps I'll head over to the zoo now. Mum used to sing a great song about zoos...

"I'm going to the zoo, zoo, zoo. I'm going to eat poo, poo, poo!"